Dear Parents:

Congratulations! Your child is taking the first steps on an exciting journey. The destination? Independent reading!

STEP INTO READING® will help your child get there. The program offers five steps to reading success. Each step includes fun stories and colorful art or photographs. In addition to original fiction and books with favorite characters, there are Step into Reading Non-Fiction Readers, Phonics Readers and Boxed Sets, Sticker Readers, and Comic Readers—a complete literacy program with something to interest every child.

Learning to Read, Step by Step!

P9-CEJ-142

Ready to Read   Preschool–Kindergarten
• big type and easy words • rhyme and rhythm • picture clues
For children who know the alphabet and are eager to begin reading.

Reading with Help   Preschool–Grade 1
• basic vocabulary • short sentences • simple stories
For children who recognize familiar words and sound out new words with help.

Reading on Your Own   Grades 1–3
• engaging characters • easy-to-follow plots • popular topics
For children who are ready to read on their own.

Reading Paragraphs   Grades 2–3
• challenging vocabulary • short paragraphs • exciting stories
For newly independent readers who read simple sentences with confidence.

Ready for Chapters   Grades 2–4
• chapters • longer paragraphs • full-color art
For children who want to take the plunge into chapter books but still like colorful pictures.

STEP INTO READING® is designed to give every child a successful reading experience. The grade levels are only guides; children will progress through the steps at their own speed, developing confidence in their reading. The F&P Text Level on the back cover serves as another tool to help you choose the right book for your child.

Remember, a lifetime love of reading starts with a single step!

For Paddywack and his Jane
—S.S.

For Carole . . . always there
whenever we need you. Thank you.
—D.H.

Text copyright © 2010 by Stephanie Spinner
Cover art and interior illustrations copyright © 2010 by Daniel Howarth

Visit us on the Web!
StepIntoReading.com
randomhousekids.com

Educators and librarians, for a variety of teaching tools, visit us at
RHTeachersLibrarians.com

Library of Congress Cataloging-in-Publication Data
Spinner, Stephanie.
Paddywack / by Stephanie Spinner ; illustrated by Daniel Howarth. — 1st ed.
   p.   cm. — (Step into reading. Step 3 book)
Summary: Paddywack is a spunky pony who jumps, trots, and walks beautifully, as long as his rider remembers his treats.
ISBN 978-0-375-86186-4 (pbk.) — ISBN 978-0-375-96186-1 (lib. bdg.) —
ISBN 978-0-307-77156-8 (ebook)
[1. Ponies—Fiction. 2. Ponies—Training—Fiction.] I. Howarth, Daniel, ill. II. Title.
PZ7.S7567Pad 2010   [Fic]—dc22   2009005040

Printed in the United States of America   15 14 13 12 11 10 9 8

This book has been officially leveled by using the F&P Text Level Gradient™ Leveling System.

Paddywack

by Stephanie Spinner
illustrated by Daniel Howarth

Random House 🏠 New York

My name is Paddywack.

I am nine hands high.

That is a very good size

for a pony like me.

I am just the right size

for my girl, Jane.

When I first got Jane,

she did not know how to ride.

She jerked my reins.

She fell off me

for no good reason.

Worst of all,

she forgot my treats.

"She has a lot to learn,"

I told my friend Carol.

"You'll teach her," said Carol.

Carol is one smart cat.

I was not Jane's only teacher.

Miss Lolly helped.

She said the words "Focus, Jane!

Heels down, down, down!"

I did the rest—

a steady walk,

a smooth trot,

a gentle canter.

Jane's riding got better.

"She's starting to feel like a girl,"
I told Carol. "Not a sack of carrots."

"Is that because she's a better rider?"
asked Carol.

"Or because she's giving you
treats?"

Carol knows me very well.

One sunny day,

Jane was ready

to start jumping.

Miss Lolly set up the cross-rails.

Jumping is hard work.

After our first lesson,

I waited for my treat.

But Jane forgot it.

"I do not forget how to walk

or trot or jump," I told Carol later.

"How could she forget my treat?"

Carol licked her paws.

"Maybe you can remind her," she said.

Maybe I could.

The next day,

we jumped some more.

Jane did not stay on me very well.

She was not happy.

Neither was Miss Lolly.

Jane forgot my treats.

She also forgot to close my stall door.

I decided to go for a walk.

The chickens got in my way,

so I chased them.

I went swimming in the pond.

I scared the frogs.

The garden was full of tasty nibbles.

I jumped over the fence

to eat them all.

Jane found me there.

"Paddywack!" she cried.

"What are you doing?"

Silly question! I thought,
and I ran away.
Jane ran after me—
out of the garden,
past the chicken coop,
and around the pond.

Jane could not catch me.

But Miss Lolly could.

That was the end of my walk.

"Paddywack, you are

a very naughty pony!" she said.

"And you," she told Jane,

"are a forgetful girl.

You must always remember

to close Paddy's stall."

A little later, Jane came to my stall.

"Paddywack," she said,

"I saw you jump the garden fence.

Your jump was perfect.

It was much better

than the jumps you do for me."

There are reasons for that,

I thought.

"Let's make a deal,"

said Jane.

My ears wiggled.

I was listening.

22

"Please jump for me

the way you jumped

the garden fence," said Jane.

"If you do, I will give you

this many treats every time."

She held out three treats.

I ate them fast.

Then I gave a little whuffle.

It was a deal.

The next day,

Jane and I jumped and jumped.

Each jump was perfect.

"Fantastic!" cried Miss Lolly.

Jane gave me all my treats.

The jumps got higher.

We worked hard.

Jane gave me treats every day.

I was proud of her.

Early one morning,

Jane groomed me for a long time.

She polished my hooves.

She braided my mane.

She and Miss Lolly
led me into the van.
Where were we going?

We got out in a big field.
There were horses and ponies
and trailers all around us.
We were at a horse show!
I saw lots of old friends.
We whinnied and snuffled
and pranced for each other.

Then Jane rode me to the ring.

Our first class was Walk-Trot.

Easy, I thought.

But it wasn't easy for Jane.

She held her crop upside down.

She lost a stirrup.

She dropped the reins.

There were five of us in the class.

We came in fifth.

Next was Walk-Trot-Canter.

Jane can do this, I thought.

But I was wrong.

There were six in the class.

We came in sixth.

Cross-rails were next.

Miss Lolly patted Jane's shoulder.

"You and Paddy can show off

your jumping," she said.

Good! I thought.

Lots of treats!

Jane looked unhappy.

She whispered in Miss Lolly's ear.

"Really!" said Miss Lolly, frowning.

"You'd better have a talk with him."

Jane led me away from the ring.

"Paddywack," she said,

"I have something to tell you.

I—I forgot your treats."

What? My ears went back.

I couldn't believe it!

"I know we had a deal," said Jane.

"But . . . I messed up."

She hung her head.

"I wouldn't blame you
   if you dumped me
   right in front of the judges," she said.
   Now, there's an idea! I thought.

Miss Lolly hurried over.

The jumping class was starting.

"Jump the way you jumped

the garden fence," begged Jane.

"Please, Paddy!"

I am a pony with a good heart.

I decided to help Jane.

When the judge called, "Walk,"

I moved evenly

so Jane could sit up tall.

When she called, "Trot!"

my trot was as smooth as ribbon silk.

Then came the cross-rail.

I pretended I was jumping

the garden fence.

Jane kept her head up

and her heels down.

We were perfect.

Miss Lolly gave us a thumbs-up.

So did the judge.

When we got home,

Jane gave me more treats

than I could count.

Then she brushed me

and kissed me

and rubbed my nose.

"Paddywack," she said,

"you are the best pony in the world.

I will never, *ever*

forget your treats again."

And she didn't.